For Cameron
~ L.J.

For Peter John
~ J.C.

© 1997 by LITTLE TIGER PRESS
An imprint of Magi Publications, London

This 2010 edition published by Sandy Creek,
by arrangement with LITTLE TIGER PRESS

Text copyright © Linda Jennings 1997
Illustrations copyright © Jane Chapman 1997
Linda Jennings and Jane Chapman have asserted their
rights to be identified as the author and illustrator of this work
under the Copyright, Designs and Patents Act, 1988.

Sandy Creek, 122 Fifth Avenue, New York, NY 10011

ISBN 978-1-4351-2534-6

Printed and bound in China

1 3 5 7 9 10 8 6 4 2

Penny and Pup

Linda Jennings   illustrated by Jane Chapman

Sandy Creek

On the first night in her new home, Penny had whined and howled and scratched at the door. So her family gave her Pup to be her friend. Pup was all squashy and floppy, and he lived in Penny's basket. She chewed and loved him to bits.

One day Penny and Pup went out into the garden.
Henry the cat was sitting in the yard.
"Hello, Penny," said Henry. "Where are you going?"
Penny put Pup down and gave him a little lick.
"For a walk," said Penny. "Just Pup and me."
"Can I come, too?" asked Henry.
"Pup only wants *me* for a friend," she said.
"Sorry."

And, picking Pup
up again, she trotted
down the path.

By the back gate Betsy the rabbit was sitting in her hutch. "Penny!" she cried. "Come and talk to me! I'm lonesome."

"Pup doesn't want to stop to talk. We're going for a walk, just Pup and me," said Penny. "Sorry."

And off she went, with Pup's long legs
trailing behind her.

On the edge of the
lawn sat Matt the fox cub.
"Come and play with me!"
he barked.
"Pup doesn't like playing with foxes.
We're going for a walk, just Pup and
me," said Penny. "Sorry."

Penny turned her back on Matt
and walked with Pup across the
yard to the garden shed.

Under the shed was a big space.
Penny put Pup down gently and sniffed.
It smelled exciting under there, like mice
and old dog bones.

"Let's go exploring, Pup," said Penny,
and pushing Pup in front of her, she
squeezed her head under the shed.

Penny tried to follow Pup. She wriggled and squeezed and squeezed and wriggled, but she was too big to crawl into the space. "Pup, Pup!" she called, but of course Pup said nothing. Penny tried to pull Pup out again, but she couldn't reach him. She couldn't even *see* him.

Penny sat down and cried.

What would she do without Pup?

And what would Pup do without *her*?

Matt the fox cub heard her and came trotting across the yard. "I'll help you," he said. But though he wriggled and squeezed and squeezed and wriggled, he couldn't reach Pup either.

Henry the cat was sitting
on the fence, and he saw
Matt trying to rescue Pup.
"*I'll* help you," he said.
But Henry was a fat cat,
and he couldn't even fit
his *head* under the shed.

Along bounced Betsy the rabbit.
She was feeling happy because she
had escaped from her hutch.
"*I'll* help you," she said. And since Betsy
was a small rabbit, she was able to wriggle
and squeeze and squeeze and wriggle under
the shed—but Pup wasn't there anymore!

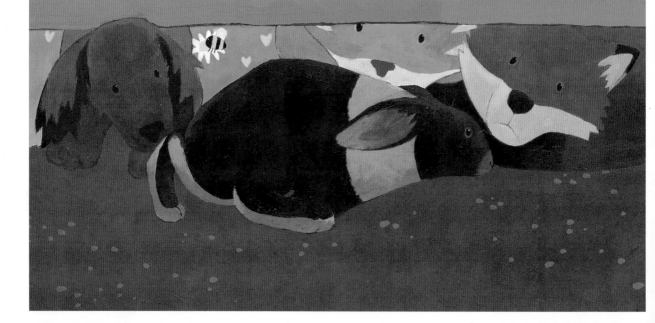

Matt and Henry and Betsy all helped
Penny to look for Pup.
They searched behind the shed.
They searched in the flower beds.
They even searched in the pond,
just in case Pup had fallen in.
But Pup wasn't anywhere to be found.
And then suddenly . . .

. . . there he was!

Pup was in the hedge. A family of mice
had dragged him there, and now they were
all curled up together, fast asleep on Pup.

Penny looked at Pup and she looked at the mice.
It didn't seem right to disturb them.
"Now you can play with us!" meowed Henry.
"Yes, do!" cried Matt and Betsy together.
"You don't mind, do you, Pup?" asked Penny,
but Pup said nothing.

"All right, I *will* play with you," said Penny, and she raced and chased and chased and raced all around the garden with her new friends. Penny was having such fun that she forgot about Pup.

When it was time to go home, Penny remembered poor old Pup lying in the hedge and went back to fetch him.

The baby mice were still
asleep, but their mother was awake.
"Pup makes such a cozy bed for my babies,"
she said. "May we borrow him for a while?"
Pup did seem very happy with the little mice.

"I think Pup would like to stay with you," Penny said. "I always thought he needed a few more friends."